SING ME
A COLLECTION
OF
EROTIC POEMS

RESTORATION OF THE BREACH
WITHOUT BORDERS

JASCINTH RICHARDS

ISBN: 978-1-954755-30-7

Published by:
Restoration of the Breach without Borders
West Palm Beach, Florida 33407
restorativeauthor@gmail.com
Tele: (561) 388-2949

Formatting and Publishing done by:
Leostone Morrison
Publisher.20@aol.com

JASCINTH RICHARDS

Dedication

This book is dedicated to Devon A. Hinds, my chief motivator. Thanks for being there every step of the way and for encouraging these poems while providing the inspiration I needed to complete them. You pushed and pushed me to write and publish and I am indebted to you.

I will love you always, my lion.

Acknowledgements

Thank you, Elvy Soltau, for seeing the talent and encouraging this book and for putting on the pressure for me to own and hone my talents. The student has indeed become the master.

You came into my life just when I needed you. To my aunt Dell, my very first mentor from whom I believe I got my love of reading which fueled my writing, thank you. Thank you to my other family members and friends who patiently listened while I read to you my work.

I enjoyed laughing with you at the appropriate times. Reading aloud to you helped me to make necessary edits. Thanks to you, Mr. Leostone Morrison, for your patience and encouragement while I work. Thank you all for having my back always.

Table of Content

Introduction

I sincerely believe that we were created by God to be sensual beings and there should be no shame in accepting our sexuality. Sometimes we find passion in the simplest of things. I started writing "The Waterfall" and could not help how erotic it sounded. A few edits and I was delightfully lost.

This book is meant to evoke feelings of love and desire. However, it is not meant to support objectophilia as it was inspired by a real person. I recommend reading it with a partner. The intention is for you to enjoy reading these poems as much as I enjoyed writing them for your pleasure.

Section 1

Nature's Passion

There are so many aspects of nature that can stimulate us sexually: a droplet of water, a tickle from a

leaf, a gentle touch of wind or even skinny dipping in a cold body of water. Let nature excite you and

take you to the edge.

The Waterfall

I am in awe of your imposing size

Hovering above me.

I feel myself shiver

As you produce ripples

All over my body

When touched by the gift of life
cascading down

Your slick wall.

I breathe in the freshness of your morning
scent

And crane my neck to capture your peak.

I am envious of the women who bare their
bodies

For you daily.

Climbing up,

Then sliding down your slippery
length,

Soaking wet from your depth.

SING ME: A COLLECTION OF EROTIC POEMS

I grip the hardness at your base

And while your soft sounds surround me

I close my eyes and sigh contentedly

As I too become wet from your spray.

Gardening

The temperature is

Hot, but not to scorch,

Cool, but not enough to quench

The bare heat.

Come,

Dig beneath my surface,

Six, seven inches deep,

Then fill me whole with your seed

Within the opening of my soil.

My earth is fertile.

Grip your sprout.

Pour into me from your hose.

Let me absorb your moisture

And feel your seed as it grows within me.

The Earthquake

The power of your growl engulfs me.

An unexpected rush of energy.

This friction you produce

Through deep intense rubbing

Jolts me.

I am laid out, on my back,

Shaking from the intensity

Of your motions.

The bed helplessly quivering beneath me,

Shifting from its original position.

There is no reprieve.

I remain subdued.

My body shaking violently from

Your shudders,

Throbbing from the force of your jerks,

Your drive generating tremors to my core.

My feet are weak and wobbly

JASCINTH RICHARDS

As I lay trembling

After the strength of your eruption.

Fire

I was dark till

　You spark the fiery flames

　Inside

　　With an explosive log

　　　Triggered when you blow to

　　　　Set me free on fire.

　　　　Each tender teasing touch igniting

　　　　This fireplace ablaze

　　　　　Beneath a piping chimney.

　　　　Heat gushing through

　　　　My steamy funnel,

　　　Veiling the space

　　As in heavy darkness

　We become light

With fire.

Fire of love

I marvel at the impact of the blaze

As you reach under to shove the wood.

And you blow, blow,

With swelling cheeks, then…

It rises upward, strong and hot

While I kneel, low

Dripping wet

Because it is hot down there underneath

Sparkling embers igniting as the fire

Shoots upwards

Till we boil.

The Volcano

You stand there watching

Tall and regal in your stance

Waiting for stimulation to go bang.

And I shiver with the anticipation

Of your searing eruption

I perceive your anxiety as pressure build

From heat inside making you tremble

Within your low-lying areas

And quiver till you find release

Spewing fluid, rising hot and thick

Gliding down from inside

Your steady steely composure

Powerful force gushing

Again and again

As your life-force drain from within you.

Creation

At first there was darkness

  Just sensual spaces unfilled.

    Like God you commanded

      Spreading your hands all over

       Creating waves

Over the hills and beneath the valleys.

    And slowly I felt the light

      Approaching to fill the void

       As life starts to flow

In previously undisclosed uncharted
territories

    It was good.

    And like God I rested, satisfied.

You Gave Me Water

I ached, anxious with the thirst of desire

For your sweet water

To quell the heat of my craving

And turn my barren patches lush.

Then you whet my dryness with your
droplets

Dripped onto my dry scorched surface

From your drizzle

Before pouring over my fields

To cap my well of desire,

And moisten my parched land.

You gave me water and I am filled.

Rise

Amazed, I look on as you rise

Solid giant.

Limbs stretched taut,

Hard and inviting.

Standing erect as a pipe,

Head proudly pointing up,

Firm in your readiness,

A renewed vigour in your stance.

The splendour of the rise

Fiery and fierce as the morning sun.

Section 2

Animalistic Fervor

It is said that humans are really animals and many of our behavioral patterns would indicate that. Men, especially, often boast of their sexual prowess as animalistic.

He Purrs

The tough tiger, he purrs

Excited by this small hairy cat

That he lusciously licks

With a busy tongue

Wet and sticky.

The purr throaty and syrupy

While coming

From rousing contentment

Satisfaction eminent

As leg polish leg

And as he licks, he purrs.

The Lion in Him

My lion is

Gently fierce

Burly and deep-chested.

With dark macho mane cropped close

And mean muscles gracing salient
shoulders.

Lean limbs, smooth and rhythmic

Like jazz played from an antique piano

Display the pride of his virile passion.

He moves furtively His territory marked by

my succulent scent in

The wild woodland where he is brutally
defensive.

He delights in nesting his head in my breast,

Nuzzling neck to neck,

And nibbling on the sweet meat

His dynamic lioness delivers.

He Calls Me His Leopard

He calls me his leopard

Every time he makes me roar

Low and throaty and passionate.

When he possesses my spots

With persuasive lips

Turning them dark with desire

He calls me his leopard.

While he chases me through hungry
meadows,

When I am stretched out on my back,

Rolling over for his perusal,

Inviting his animal thrusts

He calls me his leopard.

SECTION 3

Objectifying Sexuality

Objects very often obtain a significant role in our sexual experiences. As human beings we have an incredible ability to fantasize.

My Radio

As the darkness enfolds us

Trapping me in the mood,

I reach for you

And feel you, stiff, beneath my touch.

We have not been like this in a while

As I had so often replaced you with younger
models.

Refusing to give in to your tense resistance

I proceed to turn you on

By tracing the outline of your curves.

Subdued sounds emitting as my hands
descend

Send signals of submission.

Delightfully surprised at your mounting
response,

I let my fingers roam, gently probing.

On feeling that protruding bud,

I slowly and softly move my fingertips over
it.

Soft moans convey that I have found the
spot.

The sounds are muffled and strained.

I explore once more and finally groans turn
to squeals

But I cannot bring myself to tone you down

Till I am satisfied.

Tomorrow, I endure the angered chary stares

Of the neighbours.

Mirror

Uncovered I come to you.

Brazen,

With all my flawless blemishes.

Yet you look at me unashamedly,

Welcome my touch,

Touch me as I touch myself,

Smile with me while returning

My alluring gazes.

There is no infamy,

No modest lowered gaze.

My body is always striking in your presence.

Electricity

We moved with hands strung together

Wired

By strong electricity, charged by the current
of passion,

Tethered together and infused with high
voltage.

You pull all my strings in sequential order,

Colour coding the cords of my structure

Blushing pink cheeks

Hard dark buds

Cherry red lips.

Body oscillating while we vibrate in unison

The frequency of the moments generating

Immense energy as we charge and

We discharge.

Building

Searching for the right wood

Can be a draining experience

Some wood too soft

Some hard but not enough

To stand up

To constant hammering.

Will the wood succumb to the fire?

Bound to ignite from night heat?

Will it crumble

Too tiny to withstand the stand.

Will it be too thick to fit?

The wood must be right or

The building could crack.

Read Me like A Book

Search through my archives

Pick me up and flick my cover

Scan my open pages

Lick your fingers while you unravel my
folds

Let me feel your eyes as you devour my
words

And as your lips move across, top to bottom

Gauge my response.

Prop me up in bed

Turn my pages slowly and carefully

Snuggle with me

Beneath the sheets to blush at dialogues and

Raunchy phrases that meld with
illustrations.

Read me like you read your favourite book

And gauge my response.

Dwell in Me

Like a lonesome house

My vacant spots need filling

Thrust open my sealed doors,

Fit your key to my lock

To reveal my veiled entrance.

My walls, too long neglected

Will enfold you between them

Come dwell in me

Let me feel your bold presence inside

Move around

As I delightedly accommodate you.

Turnabout in hidden exposed directions

Occupy my interior.

Fill my emptiness with the heat of your life

Come live within my walls.

Playing the Piano

Long graceful fingers go up and down

Tingling the surface

Tips gently touching

Light as a feather pushing the right button

And producing rhythm

While spreading sheets and with

Eyes close

Grooving and moving

Lessons taught and learnt

We have music sweet and soothing

Teasing out the melody

Of long forgotten tunes

Your Ship Came In

I could see it in the prospect

Your ship large, fetching and looming

The impressive length of your vessel

Coming into port.

I make ready the entrance.

Soon you are at my waterfront

And I prepare to receive you.

Your vessel prepares to enter

To dock and then unload

In this safe harbour

Where you discharge your precious cargo

Then slip out again so you can

Repeat the process until…

Camera Call Girl

You call me out

Pointing and focusing luscious lens

And I perform for you

You take me in any and every position

Our relationship secretly public

You trim me down or pump me up

You move above, below and beside me

As you click, I strip, lift legs, flick,

I will be anything you desire

Crazy dancer, unabashed lover

Just record and I will perform

You call and I will come for you

Blank Canvas

Fetch your easel and make it stand

Steady your frame to support my blank
canvas

Plain and ready for your swipes

Get your brush ready

Poise for the jab

Dip into your liquid and

As I feel your droplets spill

Shift

Across, up and down.

Control the dripping.

Paint your colours on my canvas,

Plug all my spaces

As your brush transit to precious places.

Then mark your cursive initials in my
greases

SECTION 4

Passionate Experiences

Sometimes we look back at simple experiences and find them to be unbelievably raunchy.

Conversations in the dark

Hot from the prolonged trek we finished
together

Our bodies high on adrenaline

Now like an unplugged refrigerator

Begin cooling down

Simultaneously

Breaths evening out as we collapse,

Our legs dangling over.

Edgy chuckles penetrate the night's
tranquility.

As our murmured words reach each other's
ears.

Coupled with our panted thoughts,

The night noises are soothing.

We are two, secluded, in this dark bright
world

Each totally focused on the other as we swap
secrets

We do not need the sun as love's language illuminate

Each word you speak is my soul's experience,

Musings of your heart that your lips give voice to.

There is so much life in your hushed verbal,

Leaving me entranced

As we talk in the dark.

The Climb

Only halfway there

And I am already wet.

Moisture slowly seeping

Down my body,

Reveals the sweaty, clammy, stickiness of

Our heat.

Chest heaving from our heavy breathing,

My skin red from tiny bites and scratches,

And I know that release must come soon.

I am unable to hold out much longer.

I feebly gaze up at your form above me

As you reach down and

I am hazy with need.

The process is unhurried and tortuous.

I am spent, but there is no release,

Not yet.

I can feel it getting harder,

So, I beg for rest but

You urge me on.

Your arm is strong around me,

Guiding me till finally

We reach the peak.

The Boat Ride

Perched on the edge

Semi-nude, I fight to maintain poise

With my feet spread wide

And my fingers splayed on either side of
you.

My head thrown way back,

You rock me to the rhythm of your dance

As I relax in the bobbing waves.

Gasping from my position atop you

As I tenderly power down.

I am already soaked from the persistent
spray

But I am sated as I ride on you.

Eating a banana

Grip it.

Gently yet firm.

Try not to squeeze.

Ensure its standing stiffness,

No sagging.

A slight bend

Does not suggest limpness.

Now,

Peel back the skin,

Place your mouth at the tip,

Take it in inch by inch

Nibbling gently

And slide slowly downwards

Till you have taken it all in.

Then swallow.

Eating a Plum

Wash softly,

Rubbing the smooth surface lightly.

Strip away the covering

To reveal the now bare

Pink flesh,

Exposed and inviting.

With warm luscious lips

Circle unhurriedly.

Now,

Sink in.

Taste the sopping sweetness.

Stick out your tongue and

Lick the juice running down.

Slurp

But nibble delicately.

Do not bite the core.

The Roller Coaster Ride

We move in snakelike style,

Down, then up

A bump, a grind

The thrill intensifies as

Pressure builds

The ride painfully pleasurable

We are both screaming

Speed alternates with the adrenaline

Up, down, slow, fast

Every jolt, every jerk

Heighten the excitement

Till the peak.

A sharp drop

Then comes the rush of the descent

We get up on wobbly legs.

Slow Dance

My pied piper

Play for me your famed flute

As with longing looks and tentative touches

Long before we locked as lovers

Like lively lizards

We were overboard.

The melody is irresistible

I follow you to the edge and leap

Lost in the lake of your gaze

And we continue this slow dance

You lead, I follow.

We know well, these moves, this music

Our bodies are one

Our souls merge

Allow the rhythm to move you

Your body tight against mine

Dip, spin and twirl me

Till I barely dance in your arms

Riding a Motorcycle

I remember the ride in the middle of the
night

Traffic slow and scarce

The world blanketed in sleep as I revved you
up

Hood safely in place

Since protection is prudent.

I straddled you, with a firm grip,

And devoid of caution we rode.

Several times the bumps threaten to throw
us

But I hang on and pump,

Change speed, fast then slow and again fast

Through a tunnel rarely traverse,

Hills and valleys,

Grassy and smooth, I ride

Urged on by the

Power of your bulk beneath me.

41

A Doctor's Visit

His husky profound voice commands

Me to strip and lie

I proceed to obey his placid order

It is my first time and I am nervous

He tells me to relax

And I attempt to comply.

Till his instrument approached

And my tense body fights.

I try to trust him

Though my mind urges resistance

His hands are busy prodding and probing

Then my traitorous body relaxes and

Opens to his requests.

JASCINTH RICHARDS

Getting You Wet

I have the hose

   And I am ready to screw

      It on,

        Turn it on,

        To send out the spray that will

  Get you wet

  From a pipe that is filled and ready

To burst out a release.

Licking An Ice-cream cone

Soft and mushy

Running down your fingers

The sweet messiness

A reminder of the satisfaction of each lick

Taste the luscious flavour melting between
the lips

Chewing ravenously on the curved edge

Down to the tip

Stretch the tongue out and lick

Let the tongue's technique outline the tip

Your skilled lips scope up

The running stickiness

Later your swelling tummy remembers.

Eating a Chocolate Cake

Push the tool in

And glide down slowly

Slip out again carefully

And then separate the parts

Hold firmly and bring to the lips

Sink into the mush

Taste the milky softness on your tongue

You might slide your finger in

And twist

Pop that finger into your mouth

In and out over and over

To absorb the taste of this tanned goodness.

Computer Class

Class begins.

I am perked up ready to learn the language

She commanded us to unzip

So, we could extract the package.

We started out floppy

But soon we got our hard discs and inserted

It was time to input some hard drives into
the server

Just before we got to RAM.

Some of us needed many bytes

But we all already had attachments

To our separate domains.

After a while we became detached

And were told to eject and leave the room.

Class ends.

Math class

We constantly complement each other.

At close range

I count seconds which merge into minutes.

At the right angle to function

We divide just in time to add absolute value,

And express our capacity to multiply

Figure has never been a factor

And at the midpoint and base area

I boil to infinite degrees.

The frequency seems infinite as we

Prolong the journey in furlongs.

On the edge we are even though

Till we flip and

The probability of the outcome is equal to none.

You Gave Me Water

I ached, anxious with the thirst of desire

For your sweet water

To quell the heat of my craving

And turn my barren patches lush.

Then you whet my dryness with your
droplets

Dripped onto my dry scorched surface

From your drizzle

Before pouring over my fields

To cap my well of desire,

And moisten my parched land.

You gave me water and I am filled.

The Vaccine

Edginess slowly

    Give way to relaxation

        The first squirt of liquid flowing

Before the insertion

        Gave evidence of the presence of life

        As you gently massage

Knowing any minute now you would insert.

        The length reaching way up inside me.

        Concern surge within me

        Will I be sore later?

        Closing my eyes

           I prepared to take it

Soon you poured authenticity into me

    It was over

        And now life flows through me.

Let It Last

Love me and let it last

The wonder of that love.

Touch my heart

And let my pulse beat out

The magic of your touch.

Let me awake refreshed from the pleasure

The skimming of fingertips over mounds.

Touch me with whispers of your intentions.

When I turn to flee from the intensity of my feelings

Draw me back to you and stare into the depths of my eyes.

Make me swallow hard and rise to meet you

Wet with longing.

Let me wake to the sweet sears of passion,

Tender to the touch

Yet aching to be touch.

Perfect Imperfection

You see me as you are

    Flawed, yet

      Perfect

You are clothed so perfectly in your
imperfections

And I am made immaculate by your
perceptions

      My sores, soils, scars

    Are my healing

I have never been more perfect to you

Though to the world I am blemished

   They frown, scorn, hurt

     You kiss and cherish

      And I am made perfect by you.

The Dentist Visit

He lowers me gently to the couch

Cushioning my neck to ensure my comfort

I lie back while he hovers above me

Not fully confident in my ability to relax,

When I am opened so wide

And it is in

Moving around with the feel of home

I clamped down hoping I can take it

Afterwhile it is out

And I can feel the void

Where it had been nested before.

Section 5

Routine Eroticism

Our everyday feelings and desires are always worth recording.

My Lover's Anatomy

My lover's eyes are pools of chocolate

Undeniably fixed on me

Melting under the heat of my gaze

I am made shy but relaxed

As I drown in your syrupy sweetness

With no wish to resurface.

My lover's hands are sponges of steel

Soft in their ministrations

Feeling, exploring secret places of pleasure

My lover's touch scorches, burns, calms, heals

Yet is relentless in its protection

Warding off unwanted advances from jilted admirers.

My lover's feet take giant steps

Guiding, yet following

Treading the direction of our life's journey

We have ascended hills, descended into
valleys

Dancing to the tune of just us

In sync, in rhythm, in style

My lover's lips speak the language of our
love

The strength and solidity of our whispered
dreams

With warm sensual tingling kisses

That soothes fiercely my aches

Making me drunk from passion's wine while

Tracing a path along the shoreline of my
soul's ocean

My lover's heart is a conga drum

Beating out the melody of our kindred spirit

Echoing excitement, ablaze with arousal

Yearning to possess, yet yielding

Throbbing, transcending all prior sensations

Pumping love to the deep recesses of my
receptive heart.

My lover is mine

I am my lover's

We are one.

Close the Door

Close the door.

Lock out the jealous prying eyes

Of those who wish to steal our passion.

Seal me in darkness as you light this fire
within me.

Frame me in the portrait of your arms.

Close the door.

Hide me from the world's curiosity

As I open up to be filled of your hunger.

Quiet my pulsing ache as I loudly scream
your name.

Possess me through the spell of your magic.

Close the door

Shut me in your warm embrace

Let your tender words be akin to my ears
only

Fold me into sections that will unfold my
vivacity

Close the door and open me to your potency.

Shut Me In

Toss the key

Come to me tenderly, my soul awaits

Speak love to my eager ears

Open me to fantasies beyond measure

Shut me in and make me brave with you.

Cover the holes

Let no sound escape to the outside

Whisper softly to my keen ears

Hold me close while you fill me with
pleasure

Shut me in and make me brave with you.

Do not silence me

As I loudly scream your name

My moans vibrating through the air

Search my body for your hidden treasure

Shut me in and make me brave with you.

Nibble gently my lobes

Leave marks so tomorrow I will notice

And years after I will still recall

Lay me down and apply pleasant pressure

Shut me in and make me brave with you.

I Pledge

I pledge my body, a tool of love

To fulfill your lustful desires

Radiate warmth, skin to skin, side by side

To cherish you with each touch, each kiss

To house and grow your seed

I pledge my heart to you

To propel love to your stimulating soul

Each beat silence doubt's cunning tongue

To blend blood as we entwine forms

To swell with pride at your achievements

I pledge my voice, its sound

To speak assurance to your fears

To shout promises to the universe

To silence your anxieties

With words, whispered and loud

I pledge my luscious lips

To kiss from your top to bottom

To close around your buds

To suck gently on every nub

Until you have reach unattainable heights

I pledge every last part of me

To linger on parts wholly you

To complete your incompleteness

To wander through your fields of pleasure

And fill your minutes with hours of bliss

JASCINTH RICHARDS

Sing Me a Poem

Sing me a sweet poem

And let me whirl to your voice's music

Speak your husky lyrics

In melodies attuned to my harmony

Read lines with passion's tenor

Whet my heart with melodic metaphors

Say simple similes like a song star

Sing to me, my pleasing persona

Blend your bass with my soprano

Let your penetrating hard tone hit my
highest pitch

Let your soft song soothe my heart

Fit your instrument to my words

Draw out the refreshing strain

While I sway slowly in delightful dance.

Then I too will choose

To sing you my poem

My Hips Don't Lie

My pendulum hips sway slyly

The energetic enthralling thrusts

Invitingly flexible

My hips speak the seductive language

Of my feline femininity

Listen to the vibrations they send

The peddling swing of my ware

Showing off the truth of

The virility of my motions,

In uncontrolled messages to you.

Pint Sized

My wee little size

Contradict the power of my pang

Small axes fall big trees

The effect of the bullet

Is more compelling than the size of the gun

Challenge my tininess

And I will leave you with fondness

The lower the better the reach.

You will feel the immensity of my smallness

And exudè fulfilment

He Touched Me

At first, gently, barely tinkling my skin

I writhe uncontrollably

At the gift of that mere touch

At the patent power to possess me

As your life-force move inside me

I shudder, splatter

As the tongue's intensity extends

And spreads over my being

I move wildly, in transit to heaven

Lost in semi consciousness

Through the grip on my inside.

As I feel the touch

That inspires my organs to perform

And I cry out.

"Oh God!"

Taste My Wine

Stride into my craving vineyard

Complete your visual inspection

Then taste of my heady wine

Drink your fill

Sip hungrily and get lost in the savour

As you tease with your tongue,

Coat your mouth and

Lick the lingering hint

Of the fermented flavour

Present in my production

Grace your palates

Sharpen your sensory spirit

With each swish and swirl

Swallow but let the taste linger

Then you can make recommendations.

Home

It feels like home

This comfort in your touch

This heat that makes the sun seem cold

This shy boldness in my timid trace

The fire that we bring

In winter we have the best of spring.

It feels like home

When we lie here together

Arms entwine and wrap like presents

Suffocating the wind between us

Cooling down while heating up

It's just us and it feels like home.

About the Author

$\mathcal{J}$ ascinth Richards is a teacher of English
Language and English Literature. She
studied at Church Teachers' College and has
taught at Denbigh High School in
Clarendon, Jamaica, since 2008. Her duties
there involve training students for the yearly
JCDC Speech and Drama Competition. Miss

Richards is also a motivational speaker and master of ceremonies and hosts several functions including weddings and graduations.

Her hobbies include reading, writing, singing aloud and dancing. One of her philosophies is "If you have one song then sing like an angel: If you have one dance then dance like a ballerina. Make your one infinite".

JASCINTH RICHARDS

Made in the USA
Columbia, SC
25 February 2024